CONTENTS

Years ago, in a distant galaxy, the planet Krypton exploded. Its only survivor was a baby called Kal-El who escaped in a rocket ship. After landing on Earth, he was adopted by the Kents, a kind couple who named him Clark. The boy soon discovered he had extraordinary abilities fuelled by the yellow sun of Earth. He chose to use these powers to help others, and so he became Superman - the guardian of his new home.

He is...

CHAPTER 1

POWER, POWER, POWER!

Superman felt the electricity course through his body. He had felt it enter at the back of his neck and exit through his fingers and toes. By the time the Man of Steel heard the crack of the bolt a millisecond later, he already knew what had happened. . .

He'd been struck by lightning.

Floating high above Metropolis, Superman looked around. It was a lightning storm – a huge one.

In fact, it was bigger than any lightning storm Superman had ever seen before, even back in Kansas. He had to smile. "Getting hit by lightning isn't much fun," he said. "But I have to admit, watching the storm sure is exciting."

Superman looked at his fingertips. They were still smoking a bit, but he didn't seem to be hurt at all. Superman shook his head. "That might not be the case for others," he said.

WOOOOOOOOOOOOSH! The Man of Steel zoomed towards the ground.

Even Superman couldn't fly as fast as lightning – it travelled at nearly 500,000,000 kilometres per hour. But he could fly much faster than the fastest rockets. He didn't use his top speed now, though.

If Superman did fly at his top speed, the amount of wind he whipped up would make an already dangerous situation even worse.

Right after the crack of a second bolt of lightning, Superman heard another sound. It was faint. No one without super-hearing could have picked it up.

But Superman was certain that he heard the sound of concrete crumbling.

Which direction was it coming from? The super hero turned his head, trying to locate it, but the crumbling sound had stopped. Maybe it was a false alarm. Then the noise started again.

ZOOOOOOOOOOOOOM!

Superman flew west as fast as he safely could.

The crumbling sound seemed to be about three kilometres away, in the middle of the New Troy section of Metropolis. Even before the screams started, the Man of Steel could tell the situation was serious.

An observation deck at the top of one of Metropolis' highest buildings, the Emperor Building, had been hit by lightning. The concrete had been weakened just enough to destabilize the building's foundation.

CRRRRREAAAAAAK!

The whole structure started tilting!

Superman got to the building just after the observation deck broke off.

CRUNNNNNNCH!

It was falling to the ground – with people still on it! Most of them were too shocked and scared to scream.

Superman reversed direction. He flew down towards the falling deck and passed it.

"Was that –?" a man whispered, as the blue-and-red figure zipped past.

"Yes, that was definitely Superman," a woman answered. "But where's he going?"

Superman positioned himself directly underneath the falling deck and braced it with both of his hands. Taking great care to not break it in half, he started to push against the falling deck in order to slow its descent.

By the time they were only forty storeys up, Superman had slowed the falling deck to the speed of an elevator.

One boy shrugged. "I've been on roller coasters that were scarier than this," he bragged to the others.

Superman held the deck above his head as he landed on the pavement. People crowded around him in amazement. He glanced back and forth at the growing mass of people surrounding him. "Excuse me," he said in his most calm and polite voice. "But would you folks mind scooting back a bit so I can put this down?"

No one moved. They just stood still and stared, their mouths open.

"Come on, people, move it!" yelled a Metropolis police officer. "You think the man's got nothing better to do all day than stand here holding up a building?"

She shooed the stunned people out of the way, clearing a space for the hero to put down the huge hunk of concrete. "There you go, Superman," she said.

Superman smiled. "Thank you, officer," he said. "I don't know what I would have done without you."

The police officer looked at Superman for a moment, trying to work out if he was teasing her. She realized he wasn't. "Just doing my job," she said with a shrug. "Trying to protect and serve, right?"

Superman gave her a quick salute. "Right," he said with a smile, and then he flew away.

* * *

THUMP! Rudy Jones fell flat on his face. What had made that booming sound? And where was he now?

Rudy opened his eyes. He was lying on a dirty pavement in the Bakerline area of Metropolis.

Rudy slowly pushed himself up and shook his head, trying to clear his thoughts. *What just happened?* he thought. *Did someone punch me from behind?*

Rudy rubbed the back of his head. *Couldn't have. I don't feel any pain.*

Even though he'd fallen flat on his face, he felt pretty good. In fact, he felt great – really great!

Rudy jumped to his feet and looked around. There was a bright flash of light in the sky, and then another. A moment later, a pair of loud booms erupted from above.

CRACKLE! CRACKLE! Rudy looked up. "Of course," he said with a chuckle. "It's a lightning storm. A big one!"

Rudy picked up his hat and started to walk away.

But when Rudy looked down at his shoes, he stopped. He saw that his shoes had burned off. "Well, that's weird," he said. He held up his hands. His gloves had burned off, too.

"What in the –" Rudy began to say, then stopped. He looked down at himself. The rest of his clothes hadn't burned off, but they were all smoking. He took off his coat and turned it around to find a huge, black hole in the back.

Rudy Jones started to laugh. "I think I just got struck by lightning!" he exclaimed.

An old woman came rushing up. "Young man!" she cried. "Are you all right? I saw you fall to the ground. I said to my neighbour, Mildred, 'I think that young man was just hit by a lightning bolt!'"

"Hmm," Rudy said, ignoring her.

"Getting hit by lightning is dangerous," the woman began. "It usually kills or severely injures people."

Rudy stretched out his arms and flexed. He moved his neck around. He ran on the spot for a little while. "Well, I'm definitely not dead," he said. "Actually, I've never felt this good before. I mean, I feel like I could take on the world."

The woman stared blankly at Rudy.

Rudy laughed. "And you know what?" he said, more to himself than the woman watching him. "I probably can."

The man ripped the rest of his clothes off. "No need for these stupid things anymore," he said. "There's no reason to hide who I am."

The woman gasped when she saw his bright purple skin.

"Oh, no," the woman murmured. "You're . . . you're that –"

Rudy finally turned towards her. "Go ahead," he growled. "You can say it."

"You're the Parasite," she whispered. "You're the one who steals people's energy!"

Rudy Jones nodded. "That's right, I am. I'm the Parasite," he said with a smirk. "And you know what? I just got hit by lightning – and I survived."

The old woman slowly shook her head and held her handbag close.

Parasite grinned. "In fact, I did much more than survive." He began to laugh. "Do you know what this means, old lady?"

"It means I can do this!" Parasite added.

ZOOOOOOOOM! The villain jumped up and grabbed the electrical wire above the street. *RIP!* He pulled it down and held the torn cable in his fists.

CRACKLE! CRACKLE! It sparked and hissed. Parasite winked at the lady, and then he bit down onto the electrical cable.

ZAPPPPPPPPP!

Electricity surged into Parasite. The lady screamed as sparks flew around them.

Parasite grinned. "Now that's more like it!" he said. He dropped the cable on the ground. It twisted back and forth like an angry snake.

"But it's not enough," he said. "I still need more."

As the woman backed away, three shopkeepers came out of nearby shops. Seeing the electrical wire on the ground, they quickly warned people to stay away.

Parasite didn't look at them. He didn't even notice they were there. Instead, he just walked away. He moved slowly at first, but soon broke into a sprint.

As he picked up speed, accelerating past speeding cars, he kept muttering to himself. "More," he whispered. "More, more, more!"

CHAPTER 2

POWER TOWER

SCREEEEEEEEEEEEECH!

Parasite came to a screeching halt. He glanced at the concrete structure around him, taking it all in. "Wow," he said in awe, looking up at the enormous Metropolis Dam. The gigantic structure was quite a sight.

Parasite knew that dams were used for two things. They held back water, so cities wouldn't get flooded. They were also used to make electricity . . . somehow.

Parasite wasn't quite sure how a dam generated power, but he thought it couldn't be too hard to work out.

Besides, if there was power in there somewhere, he was going to find it. And steal it. Parasite almost felt like he was powerful enough now to be able to smell it. Power. More power was what he wanted. No, it was what he needed!

Suddenly, a nearby dam worker noticed him standing there. "Hey, buddy, you lost or what?" he asked. "Is there something I can help you with?"

The worker stopped talking when he got close enough to see who he was talking to. "Oh!" he cried. "Hey, you're –"

"Yeah, I know," Parasite said. "Just tell me where the power is located, and you won't get hurt."

"Uh, I don't understand," the man stammered.

"The power," Parasite repeated. "Where is it?"

The worker backed away and held up his hands. "What do you mean?" he asked quietly.

Parasite sighed. "You're no use to me," he said. *THUMP!* Parasite shoved the worker over the ledge. He flew back and fell into the water far below with a gigantic *SPLASH!*

A guard came running over. "Hey!" he cried. "Why did you do that!" He looked down below. He could see the worker bobbing up and down in the water, which meant he was okay for now. "You're just lucky he's not hurt –"

Parasite turned to face the man.

The guard's eyes widened with fear. He grabbed his radio. "Security? We've got a problem," he said. "A big one. Parasite –"

Parasite lifted the guard over his head and threw him into the water. *SPLASSSSSH!*

"Too much talk," Parasite said, dusting his hands off. "Not enough action."

Parasite scratched his head. The power was here, but how could he access it? Parasite tapped the dam. The concrete felt solid. He slammed it with a fist.

WHAMMMMMM! A tiny crack appeared. He hit it harder. *CRUNNNNNNNCH!* The crack got bigger.

Parasite heard something. He lifted his head to listen.

It sounded like a train, but Parasite knew that it wasn't. The villain cracked his knuckles and grinned. "Superman is coming," he said.

Superman was flying so fast that the water around the dam spread into waves as he flew into view.

Parasite braced himself for an attack, but the Man of Steel landed a couple of metres away. "Hello, Rudy," Superman said calmly.

"No!" growled Parasite. "I'm not Rudy, not anymore. Call me by my real name . . . Parasite!"

"Fine," Superman said, holding up his hands. "Parasite, listen, there's no reason we can't –"

KRAKA-BOOOOOOOOOM!

Parasite slugged Superman.

The punch barely made the hero's head turn, but Superman was still amazed at the power of the strike. Most humans couldn't even bend Superman's finger, let alone make him recoil from a punch. He could tell that Parasite was much faster and stronger than he'd been the last time they'd tangled.

"Didn't think I could move so fast, huh?" Parasite asked.

Superman didn't answer. Parasite's speed wasn't the only problem. Every time Parasite touched Superman, he drained a little bit of the Man of Steel's power. Superman could feel that even that tiny bit of contact had sucked some energy right out of him. Fighting Parasite was always very tricky.

Superman had to find a way to defeat the villain without touching him, or letting Parasite touch him.

And this time, Parasite had damaged a dam. Which meant he not only had to find a way to beat the villain, but the hero had to do it before the dam broke.

Superman looked around to make sure there weren't any innocent bystanders near by. The hero didn't want others to get hurt while they fought.

But as soon as Superman took his eyes off Parasite, the villain lunged at him. *SLAP!* He wrapped his hands around Superman's neck.

The Man of Steel felt power draining out of him. *THUMP!* He shoved Parasite away and stepped back.

How can I defeat a villain without touching him? Superman wondered. Then he had an idea. He would lead Parasite away from the dam to somewhere safer to fight. If they broke that dam, who knows how many lives could be lost.

Superman started to fly away, but then he stopped. Parasite wasn't following him. He had turned back towards the dam, as if he were studying it.

This doesn't make any sense, Superman thought. *If he's not here to fight me, then what is Parasite up to?*

"I guess I'll have to go and ask him nicely," Superman said to himself.

He flew towards Parasite. Just before the two collided, Parasite whirled around. He looked surprised to see the Man of Steel rushing at him.

As the two smashed into each other, Superman threw a shoulder block.

WHAMMMMMM!

Parasite was launched hundreds of metres into the air. On the way down, he smashed into an oak tree near the dam's powerhouse.

"So," Parasite said, picking himself up. "That's how it's going to be, huh?" He motioned towards Superman with his palm up, taunting him to attack.

WHUMP!

The Man of Steel landed in front of the purple super-villain. He and Parasite had battled before, but Parasite was acting differently this time.

"Parasite," Superman said, "I don't know what you want, but I can help."

"No," Parasite growled. "You can't. You of all people wouldn't help me. You don't have a clue."

The villain lurched towards the Man of Steel, but Superman backed away. "What, you don't want to touch me?" Parasite said. "Fine, I'll stay right here."

KA-RUNCH! Parasite ripped the oak tree right out of the ground and hurled the giant hunk of wood at Superman.

The tree hit the Man of Steel in the chest. *KA-POWWW!* He was knocked backwards and slammed into the dam's powerhouse with a *THUD!*

Parasite looked up at the powerhouse, noticing it for the first time. "Oh," he said. "That must be where the power is."

Confused, the Man of Steel followed Parasite's gaze.

Superman glanced back towards Parasite just in time to see a fist heading towards his face. *I'm really going to have to stop underestimating him,* Superman thought.

POWWW!

The force of Parasite's punch drove Superman through the wall and into the powerhouse.

The Man of Steel put a hand to his chest. That punch had really hurt. *Parasite was always strong, but is it possible he is even more powerful than I am now?* Superman worried.

Parasite stepped through the hole he'd just made. He looked around the powerhouse.

The sound of the dam's turbines was unbearably loud. "Yes," Parasite said. "This is definitely the place."

Superman saw frightened workers running away from the scene. "Shut down the dam!" he yelled after them. "Shut everything down!"

The terrified workers looked up. As soon as they saw the Man of Steel, some of the fear left their faces. Quickly, they scurried to shut down the facility.

A moment later, Superman could hear the turbines winding down as they lost power.

Anger flashed across Parasite's face. "No!" he bellowed. "Why did you have to do that?"

Superman looked closely at Parasite.

Was he joking? No, he seemed to be really angry. Why now? And about what, exactly?

Sirens howled in the distance. Parasite's eyes narrowed. He pointed at Superman. "I'm not finished," Parasite said. "I'm not even close to being done."

Police cars came screeching to a halt. Officers jumped out. "Freeze!" one cried.

"Don't shoot!" Superman yelled. "Bullets might just bounce off him. We don't want anybody to get hurt!"

"Speak for yourself," Parasite said, rushing back outside. He picked up one of the police cars and threw it towards the dam.

ZOOOOOOOOOOM! Superman took off after the car.

Superman managed to catch the vehicle a split second before it hit the dam. Parasite threw a second car at his target. Superman wasn't able to stop them both.

The second car hit the dam with a **CRUNNNNNNCH!** A large crack appeared in the dam wall.

Superman put the first car down. "Make sure everyone is out of all the buildings around here!" he shouted to the police.

Superman flew back to the crack in the dam. **WOOSH! WOOSH! WOOSH!** He began rubbing his hands back and forth over the concrete as quickly as he could, creating friction to generate heat.

As the concrete heated up, it started to soften. Soon, the crack disappeared as the concrete melted over it.

Quickly, Superman blew onto the softened concrete. It immediately cooled and hardened, repairing the crack.

Engineers rushed over. "That was amazing!" one said.

"Careful," Superman warned. "It may not be safe yet."

The engineers inspected the dam. "It's going to need some more repairs," they said. "But it's not going to collapse. Thanks, Superman!"

"Where did Parasite go?" Superman asked.

"He took off while you were fixing the crack," the engineer said. "Are you going to go after him?"

"I –" began the Man of Steel.

"Superman!" interrupted a familiar voice. "Over here!"

Superman looked around. He saw Lois Lane, a reporter for the *Daily Planet*, Metropolis' biggest newspaper. He flew over to her. "What is it, Lois?" he asked.

"Rumour has it that Parasite tried to break the dam," she said. "Is that true?"

"I'm afraid it is," Superman replied.

"But why?" Lois asked. "Parasite usually tries to steal things, doesn't he?"

Superman nodded. "Or just prove that he's stronger than everyone else," he said.

"Okay," Lois said. "Then why did he commit such an act?"

"I wish I knew," Superman asked. "But to be honest, I have no idea."

"Well, look," Lois began. She lowered her voice and glanced around to see if anyone was listening. "Parasite isn't exactly the smartest villain around, am I right? I mean, he's no Brainiac or Lex Luthor or anything like that."

The Man of Steel nodded. "That's for sure," he said.

"But because he can grow to be so powerful," Lois continued, "and because he can actually steal your superpowers, he might just be the most dangerous super-villain alive."

Superman frowned. He nodded reluctantly. "What exactly are you getting at, Lois?" he asked. A big smile grew across his face. "You aren't concerned for my safety, are you?"

Lois grinned. "Just . . . just be careful, okay?" she said. "This city needs a hero. Without you, Metropolis is in the hands of villains like Parasite."

CHAPTER 3

POWER PLAY

"Why did Superman have to stop me before I could get more power?" Parasite said. "And what am I going to do now?"

Without even thinking, Parasite punched a sign he was passing. **CLANK!** He stopped and looked down at the sign.

It read:

Byrne Nuclear Power Plant.

10 kilometres.

"A power plant!" Parasite cried out. "That should do the trick."

ZOOOOOOOOOOM! In a matter of seconds, Parasite stood in front of the power plant. He grabbed the door and pulled.

CRUNCH! The huge piece of steel ripped out of the wall and went sailing away.

Parasite watched it go. "Huh," he said. "I guess I don't know my own strength."

Guards came rushing out, alerted by the noise. "Don't take one more step!" one of them yelled.

"Okay," Parasite said. Instead, he rolled himself into a ball and leaped forwards.

WHAM! SLAM! BAM!

Before the guards could react, Parasite smashed into them like a bowling ball. The large men went tumbling like stray pins from a lucky strike.

Parasite walked inside. The receptionist saw him approaching and tried to hide behind her desk. "This isn't happening," she said to herself. "This can't be happening."

"You keep telling yourself that, lady," Parasite said with a sneer. The villain walked past her.

Then Parasite turned back. "Hey, lady," he asked. "Which way is the power source? It has to be here somewhere."

The woman said nothing. She had covered her head and ears with her hands.

"Typical," said Parasite. He stopped and thought for a moment. Then he felt something. A tingle, deep within his chest. He could feel the energy coming down one of the corridors. "Man, I like this new me," he said to himself.

Parasite dashed down the corridor. He could sense the power source was close. His mouth began to water. He could almost taste the massive amounts of energy near by.

BEEP! BEEP! BEEP! An alarm blared. "Too little, too late," Parasite said, stepping into the heart of the reactor.

Two men in white coats looked up in terror as he entered the room. He glanced around. There was equipment everywhere. "Where is it?" he asked them.

The men exchanged glances. "Where is what?" one asked fearfully.

"Is everyone on this planet stupid, or something?" Parasite said. "Where's the POWER?! The nuclear power! The incredible energy!"

Both men shrank back in fear. Then they shrugged. "I'm not sure what you mean," one said. "We're shut down right now for testing."

"No," Parasite yelled. "It's here somewhere! It has to be!"

He walked towards the middle of the room and looked down. A pool shimmered below. "What's that?" the villain asked.

"That's where we put the old fuel rods," one of the scientists explained.

Parasite nodded. "Fuel rods, huh?" he said. "That sounds like just what I'm looking for."

Without a second thought, the villain jumped into the water. *SPLASH!*

*   *   *

Superman was flying high above Metropolis. He had no clue where Parasite might pop up next, so he scanned as much of the city as he could.

When he heard the alarms go off at the nuclear power plant, the hero raced there as quickly as possible.

As he landed, Superman saw the damage that had been done to the door. "Parasite," he said.

Carefully, Superman crept inside. As he entered the building, he thought for a moment he could actually feel the power coming from Parasite. "Strange," Superman said to himself.

At that moment, Parasite rushed forwards.

SLAPPPPPPPP!

Before Superman could move, Parasite grabbed the Man of Steel's wrists and pulled them behind his back!

Superman gasped. He could feel Parasite absorbing his power. But that wasn't all. "Your hands are on fire!" Superman said.

"Yeah," Parasite agreed. "Nuclear fuel tends to have that effect."

Superman ripped his arms away. It took all his strength to pry his hands free. He stepped back a couple of metres from Parasite. The villain's strength and speed rivalled Superman's now.

Parasite lunged at the Man of Steel.

CRACK! His fist connected with Superman's chest. As Superman reeled backwards from the punch, he could feel more power draining from the brief contact.

POW! SLAM! Parasite hit him again and again, each time siphoning a little bit more of the Man of Steel's strength.

The Man of Steel rolled away. Parasite ran at him, but Superman flew up and away. Within seconds, he had disappeared from sight.

"Coward!" Parasite screamed.

But when he was just out of view, Superman doubled back. He scooped up a nearby dumper truck and carried it to the plant.

Parasite looked up just as a shadow fell over him. **BOOOOM!** Superman dropped the truck right on top of him.

The Man of Steel used his X-ray vision to look through the truck to see if Parasite was injured.

Superman wanted to stop Parasite without killing him, so he'd have to be careful.

The Man of Steel saw that the ground underneath the truck was crushed and Parasite's eyes were closed. But the villain was still breathing.

A moment later, the truck smashed into the hero's head. **CLANK!**

The Man of Steel fell on his back. He sat up just in time to see Parasite's foot flying towards him. **WHUMP!**

The kick drove the super hero through a wall of the power plant. He smashed through three more walls, tumbled outside, and then landed in a lake.

SPLOOOOOOOOOSH!

Parasite smirked. "Weakling," he said.

Parasite flexed his muscles. "I'm not strong enough yet," he said. "I need more!"

WOOOOOOOOOSH!

Superman burst out of the water. As he rushed towards the damaged power plant, he saw Parasite dash out of sight. The Man of Steel gritted his teeth. Parasite needed to be stopped. But first, Superman had to make sure the people inside the building were safe.

A woman rushed out of the building. "Superman," she gasped. "People are trapped inside!"

The Man of Steel forced himself to move at a normal speed. He could see how much damage there was to the building already. If he moved too fast, the vibrations might cause some of it to collapse.

Superman entered the main control room. A huge piece of machinery had fallen, separating workers from the only emergency exit.

Superman made sure the power was cut off, and then he carefully lifted the twisted metal off the ground. Two of the workers were able to crawl underneath it and escape, but the third worker had been injured. When they realized he couldn't move on his own, they quickly crawled back to pull out their injured co-worker.

The Man of Steel got everyone out of the building safely. Then he helped the engineers make sure the reactors were shut down.

"I'm sorry about all of this," Superman said when the job was finished.

"Superman," an engineer replied. "If it hadn't been for you, who knows what Parasite might have done?" The engineer paused. "What do you think he's going to do next?"

Superman sighed. "I wish I knew," the hero said.

CHAPTER 4
POWER HUNGRY

"Okay," Parasite said to himself. "Now I'm mad."

He was walking around in his gigantic apartment. Well, the apartment wasn't actually his. He had seen it from the street and decided he wanted it. So, he broke in and kicked the owners out and claimed it as his own. Before they left, he warned them that if they told anybody he was there, he would destroy the entire building.

But now he was doing that anyway. He didn't mean to damage the building, but the more he thought about Superman stopping him again and again, the angrier he became. And every time he got angry, he punched a wall.

CRUNCH! CRUNCH!

"How dare he?" Parasite raged. "Who appointed him leader of the world? Why does he get to decide who does what? It's not fair!"

Parasite put his fist through another wall. **SMASH!!** It collapsed, crushing the piano next to it.

"I mean, okay, some people might have got hurt," Parasite admitted. "But that's what they get for not being as strong as I am. Or lucky enough to have my powers."

Parasite stopped. "I'm not strong enough yet," he said. "I need more power – I need enough to stop Superman. The world is better off without him bossing people like me around!" He looked out of the window. "But where can I get more power? If even a nuclear reactor wasn't enough. . ."

Parasite saw the S.T.A.R. Labs building, an experimental scientific facility, in the distance. "Hey!" he said. "That's where I got my powers in the first place. I'll bet they've got some kind of amazing power that no one else does!"

A moment later, Parasite exited the building through the front door, slamming it shut as he left.

RRRUMMMMBLE! As he left, the building's huge cement awning collapsed.

*   *   *

"Clark?" a voice said. "Hey, Kent!"

Clark Kent jumped. He had been lost in thought, wondering what Parasite really wanted, why he was acting so strangely, and where he would strike next.

Clark looked up. "Uh, yes, chief?" he answered.

Perry White, the editor of the *Daily Planet* newspaper, was frowning. "I assume you're thinking up your next award-winning story for me?" he asked.

Clark grinned. "You bet," he said.

Perry grunted and started to walk away. "Hey, Perry?" Clark called after him.

Perry turned back. "What is it, Kent?" he asked impatiently.

"What do you think Parasite wants?" Clark asked. "Why is he running around causing problems?"

Perry shrugged his shoulders. "Power, probably," he said. "Isn't that what everybody wants? I mean, I'm not doing this job for money or power, that's for sure. They don't pay me nearly enough to put up with you lot!"

Clark smirked. "What about doing something because it's the right thing to do?" he asked. "Aren't you working here to help make the world a better place?"

"Well, sure," Perry said. "But Parasite doesn't strike me as somebody who cares about doing the right thing."

"So," Clark said, "that leaves money or power."

"If you ask me," Perry said, "there isn't much of a difference."

Clark shrugged.

"He just wants more power so he can get more power?" Clark said. "That doesn't make a lot of sense."

Perry laughed. "Clark, you'd be surprised how often that ends up being the case," he said. "Everyone with power just ends up wanting more."

"Maybe," Clark said to Perry, but deep down he knew that wasn't always the case. After all, as Superman, he didn't want any more power. He just wanted to keep people safe from those who did. With that said, Perry was almost certainly right about Parasite. He never looked ahead or had a plan – he just kept looking for power.

"But even a nuclear power plant didn't give him enough power," Clark said. "Where else could he get more?"

Clark and Perry looked at each other. Their eyes went wide as they spoke at the same time. "S.T.A.R. Labs!" they shouted.

Clark ran out of the newsroom. "Go get him, Kent!" Perry yelled after him.

Clark stopped by the stairs. He looked around. No one was in sight, so he ducked into a broom cupboard. He ripped off his shirt, revealing his Superman uniform underneath. Clark opened a window and jumped out.

WOOOOOOOSH!

Superman flew away from the Daily Planet Building towards S.T.A.R. Labs.

As he got close to the building, Superman used his X-ray vision. The hero saw what he was afraid of: Parasite was inside . . . and he was glowing!

Superman flew over the building and dropped right through the roof, landing behind Parasite.

The villain was standing in front of an enormous machine. The device was shaking, and a loud, crackling noise was coming from it.

CRAAAACKLE

Parasite had yanked off a cable from the device, and now held it in one fist. A burning smell came from his hand where the electricity left his body.

"Parasite," Superman said. "What are you doing? You'll kill yourself!"

"No!" Parasite said. "Not enough! Not nearly enough! I still need more!"

Parasite slapped Superman with the back of his hand. *KRAKOOOOOOM!* Electricity flew from Parasite's fingertips as Superman went flying backwards.

Superman smashed through a wall – and kept going. *CRUNCH!* He hit the top corner of a nearby building and broke that off, as well.

Finally, he was able to get control of himself. "That," Superman said, "is someone who doesn't know his own power."

Superman started to fly back towards S.T.A.R. Labs, but then he stopped. "He still thinks he doesn't have enough power," Superman said.

A grin slowly crossed Superman's face. "Maybe I should just give him what he wants," he said to himself.

WOOOOOSH!

Superman headed back to S.T.A.R. Labs.

CHAPTER 5

OVERWHELMING POWER

Superman did not return to the top floor of S.T.A.R. Labs. This time, he went down into the basement far below the rest of the building. There was someone he needed to visit.

"Superman!" said an old man in a long white coat.

"Hello, Dr Hamilton," Superman said. "I was wondering if you could help me with something."

"After all the times you've helped S.T.A.R. Labs and Metropolis?" replied Dr Hamilton. "Just name it!"

"Well," Superman said. "As I suspect you know, Parasite is up in the laboratory at the top of this building right now."

"Is that what's causing the huge power drain?" Dr Hamilton asked.

"Yes," Superman answered. "He seems to have plugged himself into some sort of machine up there."

"Ah," said Dr Hamilton. "That would be the Nawstruc Device. It's very new, very experimental and very dangerous. I don't think it's a good idea to draw power from that."

"Really?" Superman asked. "What could happen?"

Dr Hamilton scratched his beard. "Well, I don't really know for sure," he said. "Parasite might simply destroy himself. Or it could be that he'll open a black hole and destroy the entire Earth and everything and everyone on it. Who can say?"

Superman's eyes went wide. "Is it set to full power?" he asked.

"Oh, goodness, no!" Dr Hamilton said. "Not even close."

"Could you turn it all the way up from here?" Superman asked.

"Yes, of course, but why?" Dr Hamilton asked. Then he realized what Superman was thinking. "I see," he said with a nod. "You want him to overdose on energy. That might just work, but it's pretty risky, don't you think?"

"Doctor, if we do nothing, Parasite is going to keep going," Superman warned. "He won't stop. In the end, he'll probably destroy us all. We have to do something – and fast."

Dr Hamilton sighed. "You're right, Superman," the quirky scientist said.

Superman smiled. "Crank it up, Doctor," he said.

*   *   *

HAHAHAHAHAHAHAHAHAHAHA!

Parasite couldn't stop laughing. He'd never imagined he would have such power! He'd barely touched Superman when he had punched him, yet he'd sent the Man of Steel flying through the walls like a tennis ball through tissue paper!

And he could feel still more power flowing into him. It coursed through his veins in the most delicious, crackling manner imaginable. Every moment, he grew stronger and stronger. Parasite looked down at his arms. They were actually glowing.

He felt like the world's most powerful being. Just then, a painful jolt ran through his body.

"Wait a second," Parasite said. "That doesn't seem right."

He looked down at his arms again. Now they weren't just glowing. Now they were shaking. And they were starting to get even bigger.

"Still need more?" a voice asked from behind.

"Yes, give it to me!" Parasite growled.

AHHHHHH!

A burst of pain silenced him. When he spoke again, his voice was shaking. "What – what have you done to me, Superman?"

"I've given you exactly what you wanted," Superman replied. "Or at least, what you thought you wanted."

ROAAAAAAARRR! Parasite bellowed, "I'm going to make you pay!" He reached out his trembling, monstrous hands for the Man of Steel.

Superman took a small step backwards. "I don't think so," he said. "It seems your muscles are so big now, and you have so much energy flowing through you, that your body can't handle it."

"You're wrong!" Parasite shrieked, his deep voice shaking. "I can handle anything! I'm, I'm powerful! I'm the Parasite!"

Parasite tried to lift his hand to punch Superman. Instead, the weight of his arm made him fall to the floor with a resounding **THUD!**

Parasite twitched, glowing more brightly than ever.

Superman could see Parasite was still getting bigger. The hero picked Parasite up from the ground and flew out the hole in the wall, carrying the glowing villain over his head.

"I–I think I'm going to explode!" Parasite whimpered in his comically deep voice.

"I know," Superman said. "That's why I'm taking us over the Atlantic Ocean."

"But why?" the frightened criminal asked. "I'm . . . I'm scared."

For a moment, Superman thought he could hear the much gentler Rudy Jones peeking out. "I'll protect you," Superman said calmly. "But only if you agree to let go of all the energy you've absorbed over the last twenty-four hours."

Parasite looked angry for a moment. Then another jolt of pain surged through his body. Slowly and reluctantly, he nodded.

WOOOOOOOOSH!

A moment later, they were out over the ocean – far away from the city.

BADOOOOOOM!

Parasite suddenly released all the energy he'd absorbed over the last day. The shock wave of electricity shot Parasite out of Superman's hands. He and the Man of Steel both plummeted towards the ocean, far below, at lightning-fast speed.

Superman had been prepared for this. He raced to Parasite, catching him before he hit the water. Unconscious, Parasite wouldn't absorb Superman's powers.

The Man of Steel gazed at the villain. He was much smaller now that he'd reverted to his normal size.

In fact, Parasite looked more like Rudy Jones – almost small, and no longer glowing with energy.

"Power often comes before the fall," Superman said with a grin.

Superman turned and headed back towards Metropolis. "Hopefully Rudy's learned his lesson this time around," he said to himself. "But I doubt it."

A long line of police guards were waiting for their arrival at Stryker's Island, the prison in Metropolis.

"Good evening, Captain," Superman said, putting the unconscious Parasite down on the ground. "I have a special delivery for you."

"I thought you'd be here soon," the Captain replied. He turned to face the other officers.

"Let's move it, people!" the captain of the guard called out. "Get this troublemaker into the cell we've set up for him."

"Well you folks sure seem to be prepared," Superman said. "I didn't even call this one in ahead of time."

The officer turned to face Superman. "We're paid to be prepared. But it's a good thing you're around," he said, pointing at the S-shield on Superman's chest. "Humans like us can only do so much to stop super-villains like Parasite."

The Man of Steel smiled. "You're stronger than you think," he said.

As Superman started to leave, the officer got a call on his radio. "Hey, Superman!" he called after the super hero.

Superman stopped. "Yes?" he asked. "What seems to be the problem?"

"A fire just broke out at the Metropolis library," the officer said.

A grin crawled across the guard's face. "Could you. . . ?" he began to say.

The Man of Steel smiled warmly at the guard. "I'm on it," he called down.

With a nod, Superman flew away to save the day once again.

PARASITE

Real Name:
Rudy Jones

Occupation:
Professional
Criminal

Base:
Metropolis

Height:
Varies

Weight:
Varies

Eyes:
Varies

Hair:
None

As Rudy Jones' problem with gambling grew, so did his debts. To pay them off, he attempted to steal experimental chemicals from a lab in Metropolis. Superman intervened and Rudy fled. During his escape attempt, Rudy was doused with toxic liquids, transforming him into the power-sucking Parasite. Now, Rudy has a new addiction: power!

- The scope of Parasite's power is limited only by the extent of the energy he steals. For that reason, the Man of Steel is his favourite foe.

- Parasite's power-draining abilities also allow him to steal thoughts. If Parasite ever siphoned enough of Superman's energy, he would learn his secret identity.

- Not only can Parasite sap the life energy out of his foes, but he can literally become his victims – right down to their DNA.

- Parasite is regarded as one of Superman's ten most dangerous opponents, along with Lex Luthor, Brainiac, Metallo, Doomsday, Bizarro, Toyman and the Phantom Zone criminals.

BIOGRAPHIES

SCOTT PETERSON got his start in comics at DC Comics, editing their flagship title, *Detective Comics* and launching the first of the Adventures sub-genre of comics, *The Batman Adventures*. As a writer, he has been published by Disney, Scholastic, Golden Books, HarperCollins and DC Comics, writing such books as Batgirl, Scooby-Doo and *The Gotham Adventures*.

MIKE CAVALLARO has worked in comics and animation since the early 1990s. Mike's comics include "Parade (with fireworks)", a Will Eisner Comics Industry Award-nominee, "The Life and Times of Savior 28", written by J.M. DeMatteis and "Foiled", written by Jane Yolen. Mike is a member of the National Cartoonists Society and lives in New York, USA.

GLOSSARY

destabilize make something unstable, or shake the foundations of something

engineer someone who is trained to design and build things

generate produce something

millisecond one thousandth of a second

overwhelming defeating or overcoming completely

parasite animal or plant that survives by living off another animal or plant

shock wave reverberation, or blast, coming from a central impact

siphoning drawing energy, or something else, from another source

stunned shocked or dazed

unconscious not awake

DISCUSSION QUESTIONS

1. Would you rather have Superman's superpowers, or Parasite's? Why?

2. Superman is a hero. What heroic things does he do in this book? Talk about them.

3. This book has ten illustrations. Which one is your favourite? Why?

WRITING PROMPTS

1. Parasite feeds on energy and electricity to get stronger. Imagine you're Parasite, except you're a hero! What do you feed on to get stronger? Write about yourself as Parasite.

2. Why do you think Superman keeps his alter ego a secret? What advantages would a secret identity give a super hero? What disadvantages would there be? Write about it.

3. What are some other ways Superman could have defeated Parasite without touching him? Rewrite your favourite part of this story.